THIS

LONGMEADOW
P R E S S

BOOK BELONGS TO:

_____

_____

_____

_____

LIAM'S DAY OUT

KATI TEAGUE

LONGMEADOW
P R E S S

"Come on, Liam," said Mom. "We're going for a day in
the country."
"Don't want to," said Liam.

"But it's a lovely day," said Mom.
"Don't like the country," said Liam. "I want to stay here."

Just then, Gail, Anna and Imran arrived. They were really
looking forward to their day out.

On the way to the bus stop, Liam walked very slowly,
hoping they would miss the bus.

The others chattered excitedly on the bus. But Liam still wasn't happy. He didn't like the look of all that wide, open space. What if they got lost?

The bus set them down at the end of a muddy track. Liam found some puddles to splash in and he began to cheer up a little.

Then they came to a farm gate. "Please keep the gate closed,"
said a notice. So Mom jumped over!

In the farmyard there were chickens scratching around for food.
When they saw Liam they squawked and flew away.

The farmer's daughter came out to meet them. "Hello," she said.
"I'm Sara. Have you come for our farm tour? Have a good
look around."

First they went to see the lambs. Liam's sister, Bridget, picked a lamb up. "You can stroke it if you want, Liam," she said.

Liam was a bit nervous, but he stretched out his hand and the lamb nuzzled it.

"Come and see these goats," said Gail. "They're really friendly."

"This one's trying to eat my hankie," said Bridget. "Silly goat."

"Time for our picnic," said Mom. She led them into a field.
There were tables and benches in one corner.

Everyone was very hungry. "It's the fresh air," said Mom.
Liam was looking over his shoulder, wondering if the cows
would come and steal his sandwiches.

After lunch Sara showed them how to milk a cow. "We normally do this by machine," she said. "It's much faster."

On the other side of the barn were some calves, lying in the straw. "They are only two days old," said Sara. "Too young to go outside yet."

"All aboard for the tractor ride!" called the farmer, pointing
at a long trailer with bales of straw for seats.

Sara climbed onto the tractor and started the engine.
"Hold on tight!" she said, and away they went, bumping
around the farm.

The tractor took them past fields full of lambs.
"Did you see that one?" said Imran. "It bounced!"

Liam's Mom saw two cows surrounded by calves. "Those two are babysitting for the other mothers," explained Sara.

The tractor brought them back for supper in the barn.
There were fresh farm eggs and home made bread and jam.
Dad bought a basket of eggs to take home.

On the bus home everyone was tired, but Liam didn't go to sleep like the others. He was still thinking about everything he had seen.

"I wish I could live on a farm," he said, as he pulled his muddy boots off.